Can I Snuggle?

PAGE PUBLISHING
Conneaut Lake, PA

First originally published by Page Publishing 2024

ISBN 979-8-89315-507-5 (pbk)
ISBN 979-8-89315-533-4 (digital)

Printed in the United States of America

Can I Snuggle?

B.B. Moses

Mommy lies in the big bed after work.

The little child comes running, screaming, "Mommmmmmmieeeeee! Why you lying down?"

"Mommy is tired, little one," she says.

"That's okay, Mommy. I can lie in bed with you. Can I snuggle?" the child asks.

Daddy comes home from work also and lies in bed.

The smaller child comes running inside the room. "Dada, why you in bed?"

Daddy says, "I am tired and want to lie down. Your older sibling is already in the big bed with Mommy."

"Well, Dada, can I snuggle too?"

Daddy grunts.

The child takes it as a yes and, with joy, climbs into bed with Mommy, the older sibling, and Dada.

The cat sees this and, of course wants in on the action, which there is no action, just everyone snuggling together and the warmth of the big bed.

The cat jumps up and *meows*, saying, "Can I snuggle too?"

Without waiting for a reply, the cat curls into a sleeping ball at the foot of the bed and falls asleep.

The dog running in from outside sees all of her humans and that pesky cat all sleeping in the big bed, and of course, she wants in too.

The dog walks around the bed and *woofs* one time in a bark. "Can I snuggle too, guys?"

Mommy sees this and lets the dog jump up into bed by the dad and children. The dog is so happy but has her eyes on the cat just in case he tries anything.

Now the birds on the tree in the yard by the window see them all snuggling in the big bed. They chirp and sing, "We want to snuggle too."

The ants in the kitchen, while looking for water and food, stop their marching and look to the bedroom. They say they want to snuggle and must report it to the queen.

The mice in the attic, while scurrying around the walls, stop and stare at all these larger beings, and they, too, wonder if they can snuggle.

Last but not least are the fish who can see through the tank to the room and wonder if they will be fed soon and if they want the fish to snuggle too.

After dinner, the mom and dad put the kids and animals to bed. It's getting late, and the dad looks at the mom and asks, "Can I snuggle too?"

About the Author

B.B. Moses is a Marine veteran, retired firefighter, HVAC technician, realtor, who enjoys family time, fresh air, and walks with the dog.